To

Laura

LOST IN THE FAMILY WAY

BY

DR. MAN

The news about Pete's heroics spread all over so his phone was jumping off the hook, his voice mail filled with offers from perspective clients; even job offers heading security teams, calls from the army wanting him back in special forces, but as for now all the calls and offers will have to wait because at this moment Pete is flat on his back recuperating from the explosions at Imperial Construction, and since Jackson was dead set against a hospital bed, Pastor was more than ready to offer him a bed at New Discoveries, and with Phyllis giving him almost round the clock care Pete was in good hands-

"That's it big Jack you rest up now cause you've done so much so many people have come by to see you, just to say thank you; they say thanks, I say I love you!"

-Phyllis has kept up this nonstop vigil speaking to Pete; he's been knocked out for three days and she's beginning to worry, except Pastor Davis knows better, he's well aware that Jackson's fighting his own battle-

"Can't stay away from us forever you got to come back."

-Davis kneels at Jackson's bedside as Phyllis wipes his forehead-

"Maybe we should call the hospital Pete should've waked up by now."

"If this boy realized he was in a hospital he wouldn't speak to me or you ever again, no he's going to stay right here so you just keep up the nurse thing going strong and he'll come back."

-Just at that instant Pete let out a soft moan as he tries his best to roll over and open his eyes and focus-

"Dam both of you look good, how long I been out?"

-Phyllis jumps down by Jackson's side with tears in her eyes-

"Not that long two or three days, here take some water."

-Pete attempts to sit up but it's a little too much right now-

"Don't go overboard partner the last thing I remember was you flying like a buzzard with its wings clipped, and you hit the ground hard brother; thought we'd lost you, but if it'll make you feel better you've had a lot of visitors all the employees from Imperial Construction, city hall, even Al Thompson dropped by."

-Jackson smiles after hearing that small tidbit-

"Yeah he ain't that bad I could see It his eyes right after I cut him loose; he still a bastard; he alright I guess, mother fuck I got to get up."

-Jackson flinches as intense pain runs through his entire body-

"Yo black ass ain't going nowhere so you might as well sit back heal up and let Nurse Phyllis take care of you!"

[Type text]

-Pete suddenly stares at his caregiver, and for some reason, maybe due to all the pain medication but Miss Boyd looked different, but he knew sooner or later it would come to him, suddenly they all jump when Sarah enters the room followed by a few of the kids from the center-

"Hi Pete hope we're not interrupting but my children insisted they come here and give you their own personal thanks for saving their lives in a song, go on kids Mister Jackson needs his rest."

-Nobody could ask to see a sweeter innocent sight than a group little kids, missing teeth, rocking back and forth full of nervous energy, but the home made tune brought tears of joy to Pete's eyes-

"Well that's all we had come along kids, call me later Marvin."

-And with that the small entourage left quietly and politely leaving Jackson wiping his eyes-

"Kids ain't slick probably want me to buy more ice-cream."

"While you were out this letter came for you by special courier."

-Jackson's expression changed very quickly as he gazed at the envelope-

"You kind folk can raise all the hell you want but my injured ass has got to get up and move!"

-Phyllis lunges forward only to be pulled back-

"And you call me and Sarah hard headed, you ain't ready baby lay back down!"

-Pete's in his own world as he slowly comes to his feet blocking the pain as beads of sweat poured-

"As you already know us here for you brother."

-Jackson looks straight forward as he slowly leaves, all Marvin and Phyllis could do was just stare in disbelief-

"Would you mind telling me what caused all, you know good and dam well Pete was in no kind of shape and you wouldn't let me stop him and what was in that letter?"

-Davis finds the nearest chair rubs his face-

"I don't know the contents of the letter but I know who it was from; his mother, I've known that boy a lot of years but I know for a fact them old folks treated Pete like dog shit, the original dysfunctional family; best thing we can do is give him space let him work it out, I'll check on him in a day or two."

Chapter II

-Pete finds himself lost in his own solitude, letters all over the floor and his desk; answering machine still full of messages nothing but a growing rage from long ago, painful memories Jackson thought long dead and buried, the real pain is that since he and his mother lived just a few miles apart that part of the hood is where all of the pain of being bullied shunned by so called friends, learning to fight because his father stayed too drunk or just gone countless days leaving him with mom a person full of revenge who at times took out her frustrations on Pete, the only way he could find comfort was to go to his own world of imagination finishing school college army much to the surprise of his sometime parents who just didn't seem to care, not sheading one tear at his father's burial, family members he didn't know or couldn't stand the sight of; thank God a knock came at his door can't say for you but I was starting to get depressed-

"I know by now you should be able to hire a cleaning service fire marshal going to shut you down!"

-Pastor could always coax a smile from Pete-

"So I won't get any endorsements from good housekeeping which reminds me did they catch that bastard Sanders yet?"

"Not yet but they always screw up sooner or later, which brings up my question you plan on losing your tan or would you care to join me at the grill for some fish because I happen to know a couple of hot women that's just sweating me to get you out."

-Jackson tries his best to shake the doldrums out-

"I guess taking a shave wouldn't hurt any."

-Rev could not resist-

"Shower would make you pristine."

"You saying I stink?"

"You ain't the freshest thing my nostrils have encountered, but please feel free use a lot of water and soap I'll wait and pick up the mess in here."

-While Pete was in the shower clogging up the drains, Pastor ran across the letter from his mother, ooh he wanted to open it so bad-

"Can't do it, my boy will tell me about it I hope sooner than later."

-Pastor tries his best to make light of the situation as he and Jackson heads for the grill-

"And may I say you helped membership at New Discoveries increase by thirty five per cent, when the word got out about you recuperating there everybody and their sister came trying to see Peter Jackson, on behalf of me and the church we say thank you, the only people that hate you is the grounds crew, grass was destroyed."

"Remind me to buy them all a plate of fish don't want anybody hating on me."

-As they entered the grill Jackson is met by a sudden eruption of cheers and handshakes form the patrons until reaching their table where Sarah and Phyllis waited, Sarah already had the orders coming-

"The special is fried perch so I know there will be no discussion!"

-Phyllis jumps up and hugs Pete's neck-

"You feeling good baby?"

"Just keep on being my nurse sweetie can't loose with you caring for me."

-Pastor can't fight the smell of fresh fish being served at their table-

"Now you two can lip flap all day only after I bless this food and we've eaten."

-So after a lot of devoured fish meat and fries and swollen bellies, Jackson tries his best to move but feels dizzy when he stands-

"Let me help you baby too much way too fast, let me take you home."

-Sarah tries her best to help only to be held back down by Rev.-

"Wonder if she knows what to do with him."

"Don't be so nosey woman and pass me some more fish!"

-Phyllis slowly takes Jackson back to her apartment so he can rest-

"I heard your place was not too comfortable so you can crash here easier for me to care for you."

-As the enter-

"What about your job at the center, your class?"

"Sarah gave me all the time I need for you here sit down back in a minute."

-Pete starts to feel a surge of emotion an overwhelming urge of feelings, sweat forms on his forehead only to increase when Phyllis returned with a glass of water, Pete slowly makes his way to Phyllis, slowly as if trying his best not to bruise a peach he cradles Phyllis's head with such tenderness and slowly kisses her, tongues hungrily danced back and forth, their bodies pressed closer together, Jackson could feel the warmth of her crotch which by now was swollen with anticipation, Phyllis drops the glass-

"I'm sorry baby."

-Pete says nothing as he takes the hem of her sundress then eases it over her revealing Miss Boyd's total stunning nakedness-

"I feel so alone, because you still got your clothes on."

-Jackson drops his cane as he tries his best to shuck off his clothes, but due to his injuries Nurse Boyd had to help the poor man down on the bed as she falls on top of him gyrating humping Pete up and down as they kissed like two starved out peasants, all Jackson could remember was the sight on her face as she raised up and he entered her to feel the inner warmth and tightness of muscle-

"Oh God big Jack I've waited to squeeze you for so long, but you should've let me take a shower first."

"No; love the way you smell right now, want to taste my sweetie!"

-Pete could feel the joy and pain of love getting the best of him and his body, but the moans, sounds of want, small muffled screams caused him to seemingly to pass out, just to come to with the sight of Phyllis's tight shapely ass in his face moving like water over his mouth and tongue on that right spot while at the same time the sensation on his own swollen member, it took a second for him to realize they both were locked in the classic position dinner for two, suddenly Phyllis's movements became more erratic as she released a sudden gush of orgasmic juices, while at the same time Pete's inner thighs drew tight only to pulsate and send his passion squirting at the same time, leaving two naked

[Type text]

souls wrapped together in sweat and love; can't you feel it? After a couple of days and a lot cleaning Jackson found himself facing a new problem-

"Dam got me in a hell of a fix now!"

-Pete now feels more obligated to protect Phyllis more than ever and since her and Sarah can't wait to sink their greedy choppers right in the middle of a dangerous situation, he realizes a moment of passion might get them both killed, after finding a chair and taking a long hard exhale a strong knock at the office door jerks Pete's head-"Come on in and I hope you got some good news because I sure could use a little!"

-Much to Jackson's surprise a familiar person from way back in the day was all smiles and talking big Junk-

"Big Peter you sure a hard man to catch these days but I guess being a hero can upset your schedule!"

-Jackson let a smile escape as he realized that voice belonged to Cheryl Smith manager of the local drug store, but she was one his true childhood friends-

"Girl, what you doing on this side of town you still rolling pills?"

-The heavy set woman plops down in the nearest chair-

"I hate to bother you, but I'm looking for some detective intervention because if I'm right there's some pretty big shit about to go down and brother it's foul but worst yet a lot of my elderly customers are paying the price and believe me the outcome for some of them is not pretty."

-The information causes Pete to rise up and pull out the letter he received from his mother-

"Maybe that's why mom sent me this note."

"How Miss Estelle doing these days, I see her every now and then when she comes to pick up her medicine and it's the funniest thing to see a bunch of old ladies wearing their wind suits and sun visors and carrying them big handbags stuffed with nothing but tissue, and they walk around looking for each other all morning."

-Jackson doesn't respond as he continues to fold and unfold the letter-

"I know it's none of my business about you and Miss Estelle but I do know you two been on the outs for a long time but she's still your mother no matter what so go ahead open that letter then after you finished will you help me?"

"You don't have to ask me twice about that but what's going on?"

-Smith rubs her face as she pulls out some paper work-

"See right here the doctor writes a scrip but it's not filled correctly."

"Seems like an honest mistake to me extra bad handwriting from the doctor's office."

"I can't agree Pete because something is happening in my pharmacy and I can't put my finger on the person or it may be all of them responsible, you remember Miss Douglas?"

"Sweet woman made the best apple pie what happened to her."

"That lady died because she got the wrong dosage of medicine but the real juicy stuff is back in my office."

-Jackson stands grabbing his cane-

"Well I do need a few things from the store I'm still on the mend these days."

"Ain't nothing wrong with the big Peter you just getting old that's all."

-The closer Pete and Cheryl got to the store, a lot of bad memories begin to flood Jackson's mind, being the only kid in he crowd with no money to buy a snack because he was told a flat out you don't need that junk and you'd better have your ass in this house by time dinner's ready, some call that tough love to me it's just tough, but all that changed when Jackson finally sat down in Smith's office and gazed at her records-

"Big payouts from Medicare and I mean some huge extra-large money, but on paper it looks legal but for the amount coming in verses the medicine going out don't match, oh yeah there's a problem, but what can I do you should call the feds."

"I did kept putting me on hold just to send me a letter saying everything's fine, Pete I'm telling you I got old folk dying around me and I can't stop it, I need you man help me!"

-Jackson stares at his old friend only to notice a tear coming from her eye, they both snap out when they hear a noise come from the back of the store-

"Must be the guy delivering sodas, back in a few."

-As Smith rounds to corner she comes face to face with a 357 magnum being held by a nylon faced crook-

"Alright shut your dam big mouth and give up the money!"

-Instead of doing what she was told Cheryl just stares at the would-be robber-

"Frank Johnson I know you got to have more sense trying to rob this store go to jail for the little chump change I keep in here, besides ugly as you are one pair of stockings ain't about to hide all that, you should've put on four or five!"

-Pete hears the commotion as he eases his way around to opposite side of the store only to see Cheryl with the intruder facing her, but seeing Pete sneaking up, she knew to keep Johnson talking-

"Told your big ass for the last time, give me the cash or I will fuck you up!"

-Jackson slides and creeps his way up behind the gun wielding young man instantly putting him in a chock hold while at the same time knocking the gun from his grip-

"Hold on to that son of a bitch big Peter I'm calling the cops!

-The young man flips Jackson over but Pete holds on causing Johnson to flip over knocking over a display rack of supplies-

"Don't worry about that shit I'll pick it up, stomp that ass big Peter!"

-The intruder tries his best to break free only causing Jackson to squeeze harder around his neck -

[Type text]

"Wish you'd hurry up and go to sleep because I'm getting tired!"

-Slowly the crooks resistance begins to slow until he's out cold, all Jackson could do was roll over trying his best to breath, Cheryl runs and helps Pete up, she also makes lite of the situation-

"Just in case you're wondering I have muscle rub on sale this week!"

Chapter III

-As police take over the scene of the attempted robbery, Cheryl tries her best to sooth Jackson's pain-

"That was a good thing you did saving all those people trapped at that construction site, not to mention the fact you almost getting killed in the process, but this muscle rub won't help you man you still feel busted up on the inside, you need a doctor!

-Pete hears the words being spoken, but the intense pain almost causes him to see the words fall slowly towards the floor-

"I'll be alright, just needed a little rest, and no excitement."

-Cheryl frowns as she tries her best to massage only to feel a lot of damage, but she quickly recovers when Al Thompson enters the store-

"I should've known you had to be on the scene which comes as a surprise to me considering the last time I saw you my friend yo ass was barely living!"

-Cheryl suddenly drops Jackson's arm then proceeds to push up on Thompson-

"Good afternoon captain as you can see me and big Peter got everything under control."

-Jackson slowly turns and stares at his so-so caregiver-

"Lucky I to be in the right place, speaking of being in the right place me might need your help with a small problem, now only if Miss Smith would be so kind to let you see a few records...Cheryl!!"

-Smith then comes back to reality without taking her eyes off Thompson-

"I hope you find my notes a big help captain if not I'll be glad to offer my services, anytime please!"

-Al covers his mouth as he doesn't want to laugh in Cheryl's face, but as he reads the records, his expression quickly changes-

"I've heard of this; been doing police work a long time, and until recently I consider you a friend, so please take my advice don't get involved Pete, this problem is way too big I've seen too many good men and women turned up lost or dead over this!"

-Jackson couldn't believe what he was being said to him-

[Type text]

"You mean to stand there and tell me…."

"I'm asking you, as a friend please don't get mixed up in this one; besides I don't have that many friends, want to keep a few around!"

-Jackson frowns at the advice he receives from Thompson-

"Thanks for looking out for me but I'm afraid my own mother could end up being a victim, sorry baby can't let this one go."

-As Thompson starts to leave Cheryl almost blocks his way out-

"If there's anything I can do just call me anytime."

-Smith falls against the wall as Jackson slowly gets up-

"That man really gets my hair to grow, and just where do you think…"

"I got to get it together pick up Rev and check on mama, but for now all I can say for now is thank you."

-Smith walks Pete out through miles of crime scene tape-

"Be strong big Peter, when you see Miss Estelle tell her I miss seeing her."

-Pete's mind is about to explode with what little information given to him, only fact being this was a federal matter and Thompson definitely knew something, and saving the best for last his mom was sure to be a dear, but as for now he needed to find Pastor Davis, but first he needed to rest his body, cause Jackson knew things were about to get real nasty real fast,

-While at the same time Sarah and Pastor return to his office after an early lunch only to find the air conditioning system out-

"I won't have to worry about putting on any weight I'll just sweat it off!"

-Davis ignores the complaints from Sarah as he opens the nearest window-

"Come over here and catch this breeze while I call a repairman."

-As Davis talks with a technician, at once his nose picks up the smell of Sarah's perfume, a scent he's been breathing all day but only this time it was different, mixed with other body oils and sweat, yes Miss Sarah was radiating her longing for attention to pastor, only she wasn't aware of the pressure growing inside of Rev, a pain he thought long since over with but seeing the stains of moisture getting larger on the rear of Sarah's pants was more than he could stand, as he approaches Sarah turns only to see a look not seen in years-

"What took you so long, you know I been needing you inside me for so long!"

-Pastor keeps his silence as he picks up Sarah then proceeds towards his desk knocking everything on the floor-

[Type text]

"I hope you locked the door because it's about to get a little greasy in here!"

-Still keeping a vigil of silence Pastor then proceeds to pull Sarah's pants off revealing wet swollen mature woman, the unbridled smell was more than he could stand and he begins to slowly taste layers of skin while at the same time cupping both hands full of well-developed hips, slowly tracing his tongue from top all the way to the bottom, by this time Sarah was losing it-

"I need to ride you for about five minutes then I'm going to drown you!"

-They change places on the desk with Sarah pulling Rev's pants off to reveal a shaft bulging only because of being deprived, Sarah had no problem climbing on top and lowering herself all the way down only to lean forward and greedily kiss Pastor, then as quickly as it began they both groan as waves of orgasmic juices began to collect on the desk, the only thing left for both of them was to stare at each other, until the phone rings snapping Rev out of his state of relief and guilt-

"Hello New Discoveries; oh yes, well go ahead and do what needs to be done because we have a program set for this weekend, let me apologize for me not being in my office a while ago, that's alright, thank you and just mail the bill."

-Sarah's eyes pop out-

"You think he heard us?"

"Don't matter now what's done is done just

be quiet and kiss me!"

-Two souls lost in a sea of sweat, passion and denial, way too much denial-

CHAPTER IV

-Pete had to muster all the strength he could find to see his mother all he knew for sure Pastor would have to be his shoulder to lean on, no matter if his heart was about to explode sweat pouring from every orifice on his body, just the fact that Davis was about to enter his car made this day's journey a lot more tolerable, only to his surprise, Rev enters the car and says nothing, just looking straight ahead and not saying a word-

"You keeping straight these days brother?"

-Pete gets no reply-

"It's only fair that I warn you about mama she don't mind talking big shit and don't care who hears it."

-Slowly Davis looks up and exhales real hard-

"I had an encounter with Sarah."

-Jackson didn't hear at first-

"You two had a fight; wait a second, you mean to say, can't be!"

"I'm afraid I caught the scent literally, a moment of human pleasure, is causing me to have feelings of betrayal."

"None of my business really but just tell me who did you betray, I mean it's no secret you and Sarah still love each other so what's the big deal?"

"All my years of work coming from nothing but pure faith, the church my congregation they all believe in me."

-Jackson twist his mouth hard as he continues to console his friend-

"I'm not a very religious person, but you think on this, you may have been through the bible but has the bible been through you; think about it!"

-That statement causes Pastor's head to quickly turn and stare oddly at Pete-

"You're probably right old buddy and trust me this is one conversation we have to finish!"

-Jackson's hands begin to shake as they pull up into Ms. Estelle's driveway Pastor rubs his shoulder to comfort him-

"Just go in and give your mother a big hug and I promise all will be well."

-As they both enter, Pete is all most immediately taken back to almost constant arguments being forced to sit and listen, being told stay there you'll learn something about handling woman folk then sneaking out the back door to climb the nearest tree and dream of a loving home; but that all came to an end when the sound of Ms. Estelle's voice shattered the silence-

"Bout time you got your slow ass here, what do I got to do fall out in the middle of the fucking street to get your narrow butt over here to check on me; just like your daddy not worth a pinch of bullshit!

-Davis's mouth falls wide open as Jackson shakes off his mother's barrage of insults leans over and plants an innocent peck on her cheek-

"Save that slob for your woman wait a minute, I recognize your buddy, you the preacher from New Discoveries."

-Pastor gathers up his lip to offer a reply-

"Yes mam Pastor Marvin Davis and let me be the first to offer you an invitation to attend services."

-Ms. Estelle adjusts her glasses to get a better look at Rev-

"Boy you ain't nothing but a nickel slick jack leg preacher all you want is money, mess around wasting my time listening to you end up in hell frying like a sausage!"

-Davis slowly turns and stares at Pete who by now is covering his eyes and shaking his head-

"But I must say for sure I do need your help, I can't put my finger on it for sure but my friends including me have noticed something real funny going on at the drug store lord poor Cheryl bout to have a fit, I'm almost scared to go down there, let me also say I'm sorry for acting like a crabby old lady.

-Miss Estelle stands and stares at her son opens her arms-

"I'm sorry my son, but I do love you I'm proud to have you for a son!"

-Tears flowed as Jackson embraces his mother, even pastor felt a stinging as he witnessed lost love found as Estelle wipes tears from her baby's face then plants a kiss-

[Type text]

"Now I want both of you to find out what's going on and remember I don't want no half stepping and I don't take no shit either!"

-With that stern warning both men reply at the same time-

"Yes mam!"

-Driving back was more of a thrill but now Pete's mind was racing towards solving the problem, but his main focus was Al Thompson's warning not to interfere he knew something and this only caused Jackson's curiosity to spike, at the same time Rev had a big smile on his face-

"Just when thoughts of defeat had entered my soul, your mother has given me a sermon; you ok brother?"

"Something is more than rotten, and Thompson is really holding out, there's nothing left to do except call the news."

-Pastor gives Jackson a 'what the hell' look-

"Let me dig some of this wax from my ear but it sounded to me like you said call the news."

"Got no choice man I'm dead in the water grabbing for worn out ropes show my face, let the perpetrators know that I'm sniffing trust me, they will come."

-Davis frowns-

"Just hope they don't take the long way around getting to you."

-Pete cuts his eyes towards Davis-

"Don't tell me you smelling fear man."

"Trouble stinks so let's just say my sinuses love strange fragrances, more words for my sermon."

-They both glare at each other and laugh but Pete was dead serious about calling the local news but at the same time he knew that whoever was behind this might come after his friends; but he knew it was a chance that was inevitable plus it seems that after all these years he and his mother have an understanding he only knows there's no way he can stop now, but he will keep everyone safe so for now all he can do is lay back and let trouble find him, so after waiting a few days he gives station Wnosi a call, this was going to be the answer to newsman Carl Andrews prayers-

"Andrews here; yes Mister Jackson, I'd love an interview you set the time and the place; yes sir I'll be there and thank you!"

-The young reporter couldn't hold it –

"The light has finally shined down on me!"

-His co-workers think he's popped his cork the only person brave enough to approach him was his video technician John-

"Now they do have medication for this you don't have to suffer!"

"Johnny my boy pack up the van we have a date to interview Pete Jackson!"

-His partner snickers then falls into a full belly laugh as the entire office slowly gathers in closer around his cubicle-

"That man don't give nobody an interview besides he's running hot right now he could be the next governor of the state so now you swearing up and down he called here and volunteered for an interview
-Andrews could only smile and point towards the van, forcing John to comply-

CHAPTER V

-It was fortunate that Pete's office was cleaned because soon it was full of cable lights and news people straining to get everything perfect because they knew this could be the story of the century, only thing all this really bothered Jackson, even harder keeping Phyllis away because keeping her face away from the camera was top priority. With all the excitement all the makeup artist's constant arguing was making Pete sick but on the other hand Rev was handling it all like an old pro-

"Maybe this was a bad idea after all..."

-Jackson's words fell short after he almost got a mouth full of makeup powder while at the same time peeking over just to see Pastor getting his grey touched up only to be reminded by Andrews-

"You gentlemen ready to start cause I get the feeling that Mister Jackson has just about had all he can stand."

-Pete cuts his eyes hard towards the reporter-

"You got more sense than I gave you credit of having!"

"That's why I'm number one in my field just like you're the same in yours, shall we begin?"

-All the lights positioned last details made-

"Ready, one two three, Hi Carl Andrews here with private detective Pete Jackson along with Pastor Marvin Davis of New Discoveries Church;

Mister Jackson has been so kind to invite our crew over for an interview something he rarely does and for that we all thank him!"

-As the camera zooms in on Pete, Sarah and Phyllis are glued watching their men on the screen-

"You wait till I see Marv, he didn't even mention nothing to me about this!"

-Phyllis rubs her arm-

"Pete never said anything to me either, but my inner nerves tells me it's got something to do with all the stuff that went down at the drug store the other week."

-Sarah eases back in her chair-

"I forgot about that, as for that store, it's got a bad reputation for giving the wrong medicine or the wrong amount, some folk have died I hear!"

[Type text]

"Now Mister Jackson your exploits have become talk of the town including your latest concerning the murder of the Mayor only to discover the assailant to be the city manager, not to mention you almost getting killed in the process of rescuing a group of people one being Al Thompson captain of the police force;

You lead a rather interesting life Mister Jackson care to comment?"

-With a cold stare-

"First let me say if this man wasn't at my side I wouldn't be here."

"You're of course referring to Pastor Davis, strange for some reason you don't strike me as being a religious man."

-Jackson slowly turns in his chair-

"God works undercover so you really can't say who does what for whom."

 -Phyllis jumps and screams-

"Set him straight baby don't let him bullshit you!"

-So Pastor Davis how do fit into this?"

"Me and Pete have been together a long time, let's just say when the world turned its back on us we propped each other up, kept positive feelings going."

 "Pastor is it also true you help Mister Jackson on certain cases?"

"Of course why do you ask?"

"To me it just seems you being a preacher helping with detective work seems a little out of place for you."

-Rev takes his time-

"A good shepherd finds his sheep instead of the sheep finding him!"

-Sarah jumps also gives Phyllis a high five-

"My baby tells it like it is, he puts it down and they can't stand it!"

-Suddenly Phyllis starts to look at Sarah in an odd way, but says nothing because she already knows what has taken place between them, while at the same time beads of sweat begin to form on Andrew's face as he begins to realize these men are no joke, the interview continues-

 "Now Mister Jackson, can I be so bold as to inquire on your latest case?"

-With that Pete leans forward stares right into the camera and unloads-

 "It's about time because you were beginning to bore the hell out of me; the ongoing problems at Central Drug Store were brought to my attention recently and I find it rather odd that medication has been mislabeled wrong amounts or worst the wrong medicine given out which has resulted in a few questionable deaths, a few people that I have known my entire life; but the real funny thing being all the paper work seems to be in order."

[Type text]

"So I would guess that since the majority of the stores patrons are elderly the Medicare payments would be huge!"

-Jackson smiles at Andrews-

"Now you getting it; somebody's getting rich and a lot of lives are in danger!"

"That's a strong accusation..."

-Before the reporter could finish his statement Pete and Rev pulled off their microphones got up and walked off and out leaving a stunned crew looking crazy at each other-

"Be sure to clean up this mess and lock the door on your way out."

-The only thing Andrews could do was-

"And that was Mister Pete Jackson telling us about the problems at Central Drugs. This has been Carl Andrews, Wnosi news."

-Rev couldn't help but laugh at the scene that had just taken place-

"You is one mean cold dude, you think It worked?"

"Hard to say, too early yet trust me if the bastards got a flat screen, we got them wondering!"

-As Jackson and Pastor started to leave, a faint echo causes Pete to freeze-

"What's the problem brother?"

-Jackson says nothing, he just stares in all directions-

"That was an echo I haven't heard since leaving the army."

-Before Pastor could respond the left rear tire on Jacksons car explodes followed by the sound of a bullet ricocheting-

"What the hell was that?"

-Pete continues to scan the roof tops-

"Sniper round, whoever the trigger is could be over a mile away!"

-Another echo-

"So to make a long story real short; we dead!"

-At that moment the round goes through rear door coming out the other side, while at the same time all of the station crew begins to file out of Jackson's office-

"Get your asses down!"

-The startled crew stares at each other; another echo, this shot hit between Andrews and Johnny his cameraman causing everybody to scramble for cover-

[Type text]

"Don't move Rev; if the son of a bitch wanted to kill us, trust me we'd already be dead!"

-While all this was going on the entire incident was being captured Andrew's cameraman while the sound of the police could be heard getting closer, a sound that Rev was glad to hear-

"Don't get the wrong idea but this is one time I'm glad to hear the sound of our public servants!"

-Pete keeps looking around-

"Well I guess we got their attention, I love it!"

-At that moment Andrews flies up in Jackson's face and lets go-

"What kind of shit has you led me and my people into…"

- Before he could finish his statement Pete grabs his collar-
  "You wanted an interview so just consider this as being one of the perks for being so fucking nosey!"

 -Pastor soon finds his body coming between them both, they all stop when Al Thompson walks up-

"Fine time to pick a fight, but I'll tell you now I got ten bucks on Jackson."

-Pete lets go of the nervous broadcaster-

"Officer I want you to arrest this man because he endangered my entire studio crew with his…"

-Thompson cuts him off-

"Oh give me a fucking break you already knew what you were getting into when you came here so don't come at me with all this crying, if I bust anybody it should be you for blocking the street, now go away!"

-Thompson makes his way towards Pete-

"You are one hard headed man; told you to stay out of this one, but did you listen?"

-Jackson twists his lips, but at that same moment an officer runs up-

"Captain you need to see this!"

 -As they are led around the corner they come on the sight of a young boy lying on the road; head soaked with blood; Thompson kneels down close towards the victim, raising hell-

"Told you, I told you stay out this is way too big for you!"

 -Jackson's eyes stay fixed on the young lifeless body as Rev kneels to pray-

[Type text]

"No way man; you can't expect me to lay down now because I know this boy and his family, and trust me I will find out what's going down, I just hope you have enough body bags to hold the bastards I'll be sending to you, so take my advice don't fuck with me and stay the hell out my may!"

CHAPTER VI

-An endless sea of black umbrellas form a path for the small group of weeping family members being led by Pastor Davis yelling scriptures that will live on for all eternity, a grieving family looking for comfort, a tiny coffin awaits its final decent, a lone figure standing alone, scared to be among the crowd of mourners, hands tightly clenched, jaws rigid, not feeling the rain that was soaking his entire body; revenge was the only emotion going through Pete's body, even as the crowd started to leave a lone umbrella made its way towards the small hill where Pete stood, the figure hiding from the rain was Sam White, the father of Jeff the slain youth. The sight of him caused Jackson to unclench his fists and he knew this man was about to slap the shit out of him. But instead the young father smiled grabbed him and pulled close, this display of fellowship and courage almost caused Pete to lose while at the same time he whispered into Jackson's ear-

"You find them dirty fuckers and you stomp the shit out of them big Jack do it for my family, and you do it for me and Jeff!"

-As Pete watched the lone umbrella rejoin the others suddenly they all stopped, looked up the lonely hill where Jackson stood, and they all waved at him, it took all the strength Jackson had to acknowledge the gesture of kindness. Pete knew he needed to vent his anger, but a tiny voice in his inner being screamed, find Phyllis, because she was the only person besides Rev who could bring his raging soul back to earth, only thing being it seemed the closer he got to Phyllis's apartment the longer it took, no traffic even the rain had stopped and the sun was made a strong comeback, all Pete had on his mind was the sight of the boy on the ground dead the funeral his dad grabbing him and the people still giving him the respect that he never received during his childhood, finally reaching his destination he could see Phyllis looking out the window and she didn't hesitate to open the door for him not a word was said but she could tell by the look on his face; her man was hurting-

"Can I get you a drink baby?"

-Jackson smiles as he rubs the side of her face slowly-

"I'd like that."

-Pete finds comfort from the nearest chair as Phyllis returns with a drink-

"Sometimes I wonder if it's all worth the pain and."

-Phyllis watches as Jackson slowly empties his glass while she kicks off her shoes-

"Never heard you say things like that before as if you want to give up. Remember the way you kept my spirits up when I was at my worst, baby I really can't say I know how you feel but it was not your fault that young boy was killed, remember all those other people that have died because of the drug store being crooked and you know the bullshit police won't do nothing you know dam well that you're the one that keeps this hood together; babe you've come too far way too far to stop now...I won't let you!"

-While Jackson was getting spirits lifted, he didn't notice that Phyllis had made her way down to remove his shoes, by the time he came back to himself skillful hands already massaging his slowly growing maleness, soft wet lips down up

[Type text]

down leaving streams of saliva with pre cum as Phyllis rises up to slip Pete's shirt off then slide her panties down, then proceeds to slowly impale herself on Jackson; all the way down causing them both greedily to find each other's lips, the smell of love between two people wow-

"I got to cum big Jack I want to cum all over you!"

-With that Phyllis begins to rock as the muscles inside her squeeze and pulls at Jackson's penis until he couldn't hold it any longer causing him to soak her insides with semen mixed with a little pain form the day with a little case of depression thrown in for extra measure, until they both collapse holding on dearly to each other, as Pete slowly regains his composure, the sound of cell phone causes Phyllis to slowly get up as she drips the overflow of fluid down her leg, she hands Jackson the phone, and by the look on Pete's face-

"Get dressed baby we got to see mama!"

-Not saying another word Phyllis starts to clean up as Jackson's mind starts to race, because he can count on his hands who many times he received a call from his mother, the last one to break the news that his father had died, all Jackson could do was to rub the phone against his leg and think-

"I got to fix this shit no matter what it takes, can't please everybody about not to give a fuck but I will get this shit fixed!"

CHAPTER VI

-A cool breeze met up with Jackson and Phyllis as they arrived at Miss Estelle's house and of course she had that eye peeping out the blinds and she wasted no time greeting them at the door-

"Lord who is this pretty woman with you boy?"

"Miss Estelle Jackson Miss Phyllis Boyd"

-Jackson's mother embraces Phyllis-

"Glad to meet you Miss Estelle."

"Boyd, you Darius Boyd's pretty little girl?"

"Yes mam."

"And smarter than anything, now I remember how bad they did you at that college you was teaching at, baby you got treated wrong I don't care what some folk say about you, tell them all to kiss your ass!"

-Phyllis had to let go with a small laugh as Miss Estelle was just getting started-

"I can look at you two and see a nice relationship, and it's keeping both of you thinking positive; course I got to admit baby Pete didn't have that when he was growing up, learned it on his own; I just thank God he didn't grow up to hate me especially now so I'm counting on you to keep him straight, promise me baby."

-Phyllis smiles broadly-

"Miss Estelle you have my promise!"

-The look of concern never left Jackson's face as the women get better acquainted-

"I just hope this problem don't get any of you an uncontrollable case of not breathing, but I know this letter I got the other day is just the start of something that's going to make the funeral homes an ass load of money!"

-Miss Estelle hands Pete the letter which causes a hard look to run across his face-

"They can't tell you which drug store to use and to say your benefits will be stopped if you proceed to move your prescription's elsewhere."

-Miss Estelle shakes her head-

"I know for a pure fact that letter ain't nothing but straight up bullshit; I need your help son me and a few others would be much beholding to Pete Jackson private detective agency."

-Pete kisses his mother as he and Phyllis start to leave-

"Please be careful, listen to your mother son this old nose can still smell a bucket of shit; please be careful!"

-As they leave Phyllis can't keep her eyes off Jackson-

"Your mother is a pure sweetie I love her and she doesn't mind telling it the way it should be, but what's wrong with you I already know something is on your mind."

"Whole thing has too many holes in it, don't make on kind of sense, the shooting at my office boy getting smoked, Thompson holding out, only positive the bad guys know I'm fucking with them, but the whole thing just don't add up. Plus I got to keep my eye on you now more than ever!"

-Phyllis gives Pete a hard look-

"And would you care to explain that last comment?"

"We a team, Rev, Sarah you and if I know my sneaky bastards they know all of you, got to keep my family safe, couldn't stand to lose any of you."

-Phyllis then leans over to plant a kiss on Pete's forehead-

"Like you said we a team, so we be alright, because you know for a fact you can't do any of this by yourself; am I right?"

"Say anything we've come too far can't turn back now!"

-What that she snuggles under Jackson and whispers-

"Don't forget I'm a hard bitch you not getting rid of me no time soon!

"I hear you talking Miss Boyd!"

-While all this was being settled, Pastor was in his office trying his best to settle his mind because too much has happened too quickly-

[Type text]

"I got to get this boy to change his line of work before the body count really starts!"

-Suddenly the lights in his office start to flicker; Rev knew immediately what the problem was-

"I guess that's why I'm leader of this flock and that means fixing lights, where's Clarence I thought he said the problem was fixed!"

-At that instant Sarah pops in-

"Hi dear, why the puzzled look?"

"Way too much going on senior's dying innocent kids getting caught up, preaching funerals lights flashing, really more than one preacher can stand, besides I got to get these lights fixed and I know the problem has to be in the basement, so you might as well come with me cause I hate going down alone."

"Speaking of going down, I hope our little physical play hasn't caused you any problems."

-Rev tries his best to stifle a laugh-

"I'm glad you find it funny!"

"Well I won't laugh but I must admit the entire episode caused me quite displeasure, but the feelings were only temporary."

-Immediately Sarah's eyes and nostrils flare wide open-

"I never could figure out your problem, still got yourself up on this rock, figure you being above everyone!"

-Rev whips around right into Sarah's face-

"You still don't get it do you; think you just flash that pretty smile shake your butt and men just supposed to fall at your feet slobbering like a dog with the rabies!"

-Sarah keeps on-

Let's just say you did your share of slobbering, but it wasn't just on my feet, you my dear Pastor was turned on!

-Rev snaps-

"Woman you couldn't turn on a light bulb, talk about putting yourself up on a pedestal!"

-Rev finally reaches the fuse box as Sarah's voice starts to quiver-

"Talk like you don't want it no more!"

-Davis turns suddenly to find Sarah on the floor completely naked squeezing her breast, fingering her swollen vagina sending juices down to floor, as Rev almost passes out he could feel all his blood going to his feet as she puts a finger deep inside only to pull it out and lick it greedily-

"Do you think I'm nasty baby?"

[Type text]

-Without one bit of reply Davis pulls off his clothes to join Sarah licking savagely at her gushing ass sending even more excitement to slowly drip from his chin, slowly making his way to kiss his woman as his bulging manhood found the orifice that has been driving him insane with forbidden passion as fingernails dig into his tight and flexing butt cheeks only to pull him inside deeper…Once again two souls locked together, only to be scared by lights suddenly coming on, startled heads turn only to land on the janitor, Clarence-

"Uh-I just went down to get a fuse Pastor I'm sorry!"

-Just the sound of buckets and brooms knocked over as the frightened man bolted from the basement leaving Rev and Sarah drying up and shrinking up, Pastor raises up looks down-

"Baby I love you always have, but right now you make me sick!"

CHAPTER VII

-Pete figures now is the time for a little food since his appetite had been spoiled by the current events and the fact that his pants were about to fall off being held up by belts and suspenders finds his nostrils being exercised by hot dogs and fries-

"Time for a little fat in my diet, because soon if you talk about my butt, you'll only need one T."

-But this harmless food run was about to jump at the instant Jackson inserts his key to unlock his office a strong wave of electricity runs over his body causing instant paralysis but still fully conscious Pete sees his food hit the floor as he's soon to follow, now any other time nosey neighbors would be all over the place, but only to have a unknown woman stare down at him-

"An old cliché Mister Jackson I know you've heard before but that had to be a shocking experience."

-Pete was helpless as he was lifted by two more unknown men that quickly hustled the stiff detective to a waiting van parked at the rear of the building, throwing Jackson inside only to be blinded with spotlights; slowly the effects of the shock was beginning to wear off as Pete began to move slowly trying to get his brains to reboot, at the same time shielding his eyes against the flood lights; suddenly a computer generated voice startled him-

"You a good man Jackson but take a little of the good sense you possess and walk away before you or some of the people you love get fucked up!"

-Jackson tries his best to shield his eyes-

"I don't have the slightest idea what you're talking about, but does this have something to do with Central Drugs?"

"Don't fuck with me Jackson I could have splattered your brains on the sidewalk the other day!"

-With that Pete looks directly into the lights as tears stream from his eyes-

[Type text]

"So instead you killed a young boy!"

"Punk ass should've been at home, same thing will happen to your monkey ass if you don't mind your own business!"

-Jackson laughs-

"I really hate to be a pain but I will find out who you are and I will proceed to plunge my foot a long ways up your ass!"

-Slowly the door of the van opens-

"Just remember Mister super dic you have been warned; now get the fuck out!"

-Pete staggers to his feet as the van roars off into the darkness as the sound of his cell phone seems hard to find-

"What's up Rev; yeah I could use the company because I got a feeling, things about to get real funky up in this piece!"

-Jackson finds his way back to his office only to collapse on the couch staring at the ceiling-

"You son of a bitch, I will bust your ass!"

-Pete falls into a deep sleep but his mind's racing with uncontrollable dreams, until-

"Wake up before you tear up this couch!"

-Jackson forced his eyes open to see a blurry Pastor come slowly into focus-

"Sounds like you had a rough night."

"It can't be morning I just closed my eyes."

-Suddenly the sound of Jackson's stomach growling broke the silence as he stumbles towards the kitchen-

"You got to eat brother can't go after bad guys on an empty stomach."

-Pete finds a piece of chicken and tears it apart-

"I met the person that's behind all this medical scam, he also confessed to shooting young Jeff White; not to mention shocking the hell out of me in the process!"

-Rev gives his old friend the most puzzled look-

"You did have a pretty busy night, just one thing; you still alive and I thank God for that but one question that's really beginning to bother me, why did this person spare you a second time, a respect kind of thing?"

-Pete wipes crumbs form his greasy mouth-

"That's what I can't figure out, it'll come to us, just hope nobody else gets hurt, or worse."

-Rev cell phone rings-

"Talk at me Sarah girl; I'm with him now; you lying; we on the way, they just found Cheryl Smith tore all to hell in the back of the drug store taking her to the hospital now!"

[Type text]

-This was a trip Pete was too familiar with only difference being more innocent people he knew was being hurt and he was knew for sure the mysterious voice was serious with his threat of more dead bodies, so with the sight of Cheryl hooked up to life support, and the sight of Al Thompson sitting at her bed side trying his best to get some information; but the attending physician was looking down at the floor shaking his head proceeded to rub Pete's shoulder, and grabbing Pastor's hand; as the old Preacher got down on his knees to pray; Thompson starts his own sermon-

"Told you in the beginning man this was something that's completely off the hinges, you can't stop it, these bastards will cut your ass in two and throw it in your face; let it be!"

-A hard frown rolls across Jackson's face-

"Sounds to me like you're on their side, or do you even care what happens to all these people?"
-Thompson flies into Pete-

"Told your monkey ass to stay out this is way out your hand's man head like a piece of granite please before I be scraping bits of your black ass off somebody's wall!"
-With that Captain Thompson storms off, while at the same time Cheryl Starts to grown-

"We right here baby!"
-With the young lady fighting pain she tries her best to speak-

"Big Peter, I know who did this to me."

"Tell us baby!"
-Her entire body starts to shake then stops-

"Thought he liked me... Big shoulders, smooth cat, it was;"
-The sound of code blue echoed throughout the entire floor as doctors and nurses tried to revive the young woman, but with no success, only the steady unchanging sound of the heart monitor, Pete turns and whispers into Rev's ear-

"I know you got a church meeting tonight you just be sure that Sarah's there cool?"

"Sure man no problem, where you going?"
-Jackson stares at Thompson-

"Going to check on mama, I'll catch up with you later."
-Thompson slowly makes his way over towards Rev as Jackson slams the door-

"Your friend is going to get all of you killed, some things you can't change!"
-Pastor starts to leave-

"That may be true but I think in this case being hard headed may be justified now if you would be so kind I have a church to run."

[Type text]

-Pete wasted no time to Miss Estelle's to reveal his plan and he knew for sure it would be no problem, just keeping everybody safe was the only problem-

"Come on in baby, where that pretty girlfriend of yours?"
-Jackson plants a kiss as she leaves the room-

"Baby I need your help."
-Shouting from the kitchen-

"All you got to do is ask just tell me which ass you want me to kick!"

-Jackson had to smile on that reply-

"I want you and a few of your friends to get together go to the drug store and protest, I mean raise holy unfiltered hell about your medicine!"

-A sneaky kind of smile runs across her face-

"Sounds like fun to me, and I just know who to call, Lucinda, Bessie Mae, Justine; we get them dirty fuckers!"
-Miss Estelle then grabs her son's hand-

"We get them bastards won't we son?"

"We sure will baby!"
-Suddenly Pete remembered the church meeting going on and he was aware that Rev had a lot on his mind, and that church was packed with members and others from the community, Pastor wasted no time getting started-

"Good evening my friends, tonight I'm not really interested about finance, attendance because we have been watched over and we have been very fortunate in the success of this church and other activities that New Beginnings has stood behind; that's why as of today I'm stepping down as Pastor effective today."
-Moans and whispers filled the entire sanctuary, while at the same time Sarah joins Rev at the podium-

"While I must also confess to you all Miss Thompson and myself, have found love a love we both thought long gone, so we got lost in each other, and she has agreed to step down as head of the neighborhood center."
-Dead silence, as Deacon Brown stood-

"Don't mean to go against you Pastor but I'm sure I speak for the entire church and the people of this neighborhood, Pastor you gave all of us a home when others slammed doors in our faces, you gave us help when the world turned their backs on us, you put us to work when they said we had no use, a lot of us including myself would've been dead and forgotten if not for you, and for Miss Sarah when she took over the center, the children of this town have come a long way!"
-Rev and Sarah stand holding hands as tears stream from their eyes as Brown faces the crowd-

"I say let's put it to a vote, all in favor of replacing Pastor Marvin Davis and Miss Sarah Thompson say I!"
-Not one person, Deacon Brown slowly turns-

[Type text]

"All in favor of keeping Pastor and Miss Thompson let it be heard!"

-The entire foundation of the church seemed to move as nothing but cheers, applause vibrated the floor, while at the same time Jackson made his way to his friends-

"When you fine pillars of this community get a chance, come to the office it's about to get nasty!"

CHAPTERVIII

-Rev and Sarah had no Idea they meant so much to the people and the community, but they would really need each other to brace themselves because Pete was sweating like a condemned man, but he was ready to reveal his plan; right or wrong he knew feelings would be hurt; but it had to be to make things right but as for now Jackson had to figure out a quick solution because he knew the sound of Rev's car, followed by the slamming of two doors; Pete's heart jumped into the roof of his mouth as they entered all smiles, Jackson recognized the look of honest love between two people; a couple he held in the highest esteem, his only fear by the end of the day, he may lose two of his dearest friends, Jackson tried his best to hide the rage going through his mind, but he knew this could rip them all to pieces, as Rev and Sarah entered the office, Pete could see the happiness that Marvin had denied himself for so long-

"I know you two got a lot to catch up on but let me say right now; If what you're about to hear pisses you off, I'm sorry it was not meant to cause no pain, but Rev you a fool!"

-Pastor jerks around, as Pete continues-

"That's right you a big fool got a woman that's willing to give up her life and you scared what the church folk might say, and since you being a shepherd you found them guided all of them, and since you being only flesh and bone, that's all you can do, so why sell yourself short, you and Sarah love each other so why leave the church man, that is your entire life; oh you make me so sick!"

-Sarah tries her best to hide a laugh but unknowing to her she's next in the crosshairs-

"When I first met you Sarah, I got the feeling of getting my ass kicked by a mule sick with rabies, but I had no idea you and my boy had a long history, but to make a long story even longer, your son ain't worth a pinch of bullshit!"

-Before Sarah could respond-

"He came on like you'll lick my ass until I get tired, but I'm convinced he knows something, I can just about stake my life on that fact but he won't say or admit nothing, and he probably shot that young man outside my office!"

-Sarah squeezes her lips starts to leaves as Pastors flies into Jackson-

"Been with you a long time brother only this time you stepped way out of bounds on this one, you've made a lot of strong accusations but where's your proof?"

-Pete eyes them both-

[Type text]

"Remember Cheryl the manager of the store, she had a crush on Al and she tried her best to reveal her killer, all she could say was thought he liked me, and what shoulders he has, also when I got thrown in a van with lights, this voice kept saying, your monkey ass, then afterwards the next day I talked with Thompson and that same phrase monkey ass was thrown up in my face; you two have got to believe me I'm not making this shit up!"

-Jackson slowly makes his way towards Sarah who by this time is quietly crying-

"Baby I got all respect for you nothing but respect, your son knows something, he may not be at the top, but he's in on it; but if you and Rev don't believe me; I'm sorry but I got to get down to the drug store mama got a few of her friends together and I got Phyllis to shadow everybody; got a plan."

-Both pastor and Sarah stare at Pete in total disbelief-

"I'm almost afraid to ask but what in the hell are you planning?"

"Oh nothing much, just a few irate citizens venting their anger down at the drug store."

-Rev gives Pete a go to hell look-

"So you mean to say not only did you put Phyllis in danger, your own mother as well; you've lost it man!"

-While Pete and Rev were locked in discussion Sarah regained her composure-

"Jackson's right babe, I've had the same suspicions for months my son's into something but I really think he wants out, and I want to help in any way I can."

-Pastor slowly turns and faces Sarah-

"Both of you have gone stone fool!"

-Jackson grows impatient-

"We can argue this later right now we need to roll!"

-The crowd at Central Drugs stretched out the door and down the block as four elderly women inside raised hell about their medicine; when Jackson reached the scene the first thing he does was to locate his mother and Phyllis as she's found standing outside the store, she runs to meet him-

"Oh baby I'm glad to see you, better get in there fast Al Thompson's going to haul your mother to Jail!"

-When Pete entered he found Thompson surrounded with Miss Estelle all up in his face-

"I don't give a good dam who you claim to be, can take this entire store and stick it up your ass sideways!"

-Thompson proceeds to put handcuffs on Miss Estelle as Miss Lucinda and Phyllis attempt to block the way, Thompson proceeds to use a cattle prod on them both-

"All of you stupid as hell!"

-As Thompson snatches Miss Estelle towards the door, suddenly he feels the cold barrel of a gun pressing on the back of his head-

[Type text]

"You like shocking people, just like the way you shocked me threw me in a van tried to stop me, told me I had a monkey ass; now let me tell you this only one time, take those cuffs off mama and lets go downtown and have a long talk with the district attorney before somebody really gets fucked up!"

-Thompson starts to release Miss Estelle but then suddenly pushes her down as Pete catches her Al runs out the main entrance right into Sarah and Pastor-

"Baby I know we've lost time but don't get no more deeper into this shit please!"

-Her son just gives them both a hard blank stare as he starts to run towards the alley just as Pete comes out; they all hear an echo in the distance, Sarah screams as they all witness Al's back exploding in blood and him falling to the ground-

"Keep Sarah inside the store Rev!"

-With gun drawn Jackson slowly makes his way towards Thompson while his eyes scanning the rooftops, but he already knew two things one being that shot came from a distance, the other glancing at the growing blood pool; Captain Alvin Thompson was dead, and the sound of uncontrollable screams of a mother that has lost her son drowned all the other noise of the city-

EPILOGUE

-The Investigation was long and nerve racking for Sarah but she would survive with the help of her friends and the love of Pastor Davis; Sometimes trouble does have a twisted way of pulling us together, Jackson has never felt this close to his mother; and the bond he and Phyllis share was just the medicine he needed to show him that life can be worth living, even taking a vacation was something he never even dreamed of doing but since Phyllis kept on fussing, maybe a beach vacation was the perfect getaway-

"Wake up baby."

-Jackson rolls over with a smile as Phyllis licks his nipple-

"Hi sweetie, what's up?"

"This package came for you, maybe it's from Rev and Sarah."

-Jackson pauses for a second as he opens the box to reveal a laptop as he opens it up the computer starts up to reveal an eerie message-

"See what you caused; had to kill a good man because of your bullshit, can't mind your own fucking business!"

-The sound of that voice caused Phyllis to stop dead in her tracks and stare over Jackson's shoulder, as the screen comes on both were shocked to see Sanders-

"Yeah it's me and if memory serves me correct I think you were warned by Thompson may he rest in peace, now mother fucker let me tell you that death is going to be crawling up your ass, so my suggestion to you is get all by yourself because I'm hitting your ass hard and heavy and whoever you just happen to be around will die also, simple enough for you; have a nice day!"

-Suddenly the screen goes blank as Pete and Phyllis continue to stare dumbfounded at the dead machine at the same time beads of sweat forms on Jackson's forehead because he knows everyone he loves are in danger-

END

Made in the USA
Columbia, SC
12 November 2018